A MESSAGE TO PARENTS

Reading good books to young children is a crucial factor in a child's psychological and intellectual development. It promotes a mutually warm and satisfying relationship between parent and child and enhances the child's awareness of the world around him. It stimulates the child's imagination and lays a foundation for the development of the skills necessary to support the critical thinking process. In addition, the parent who reads to his child helps him to build vocabulary and other prerequisite skills for the child's own successful reading.

In order to provide parents and children with books which will do these things, Brown Watson has published this series of small books specially designed for young children. These books are factual, fanciful, humorous, questioning and adventurous. A library acquired in this inexpensive way will provide many hours of pleasurable and profitable reading for parents and children.

Published by Brown Watson (Leicester) Ltd.
ENGLAND
© 1980 Rand McNally & Company
Printed and bound in the German Democratic Republic.

The House That Jack Built

Illustrated by TONY BRICE

Brown Watson

England.

THIS IS the house that Jack built.

This is the malt –
That lay in the house that Jack
    built.

This is the rat –
That ate the malt
That lay in the house that Jack
built.

This is the cat –
That killed the rat,
That ate the malt
That lay in the house that Jack
built.

This is the dog –
That worried the cat,
That killed the rat,
That ate the malt
That lay in the house that Jack
      built.

This is the cow with the crumpled
    horn –
That tossed the dog,
That worried the cat,
That killed the rat,
That ate the malt
That lay in the house that Jack
    built.

This is the maiden all forlorn –
That milked the cow with the
crumpled horn,
That tossed the dog,
That worried the cat,
That killed the rat,
That ate the malt
That lay in the house that Jack
built.

This is the man all tattered and torn –

That kissed the maiden all
forlorn,
That milked the cow with the
crumpled horn,
That tossed the dog,
That worried the cat,
That killed the rat,
That ate the malt
That lay in the house that Jack
built.

This is the priest all shaven and
shorn –
That married the man all tattered
and torn,
That kissed the maiden all
forlorn,
That milked the cow with the
crumpled horn,
That tossed the dog,
That worried the cat,
That killed the rat,
That ate the malt
That lay in the house that Jack
built.

This is the cock that crowed in
the morn –
That waked the priest all shaven
and shorn,
That married the man all tattered
and torn,
That kissed the maiden all
forlorn,
That milked the cow with the
crumpled horn,
That tossed the dog,
That worried the cat,
That killed the rat,
That ate the malt

That lay in the house that Jack
    built.
This is the farmer sowing the
    corn –
That kept the cock that crowed
    in the morn,
That waked the priest all shaven
    and shorn,
That married the man all tattered
    and torn,
That kissed the maiden all
    forlorn,
That milked the cow with the
    crumpled horn,

That tossed the dog,
That worried the cat,
That killed the rat,
That ate the malt,
That lay in the house that Jack
    built.